0 0 SEP 2016

THIS BLOOMSBURY BOOK
BELONGS TO

....

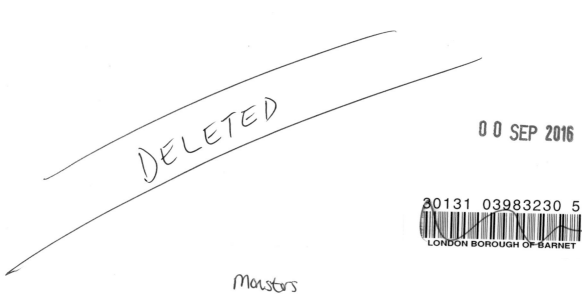

DELETED

0 0 SEP 2016

Monsters

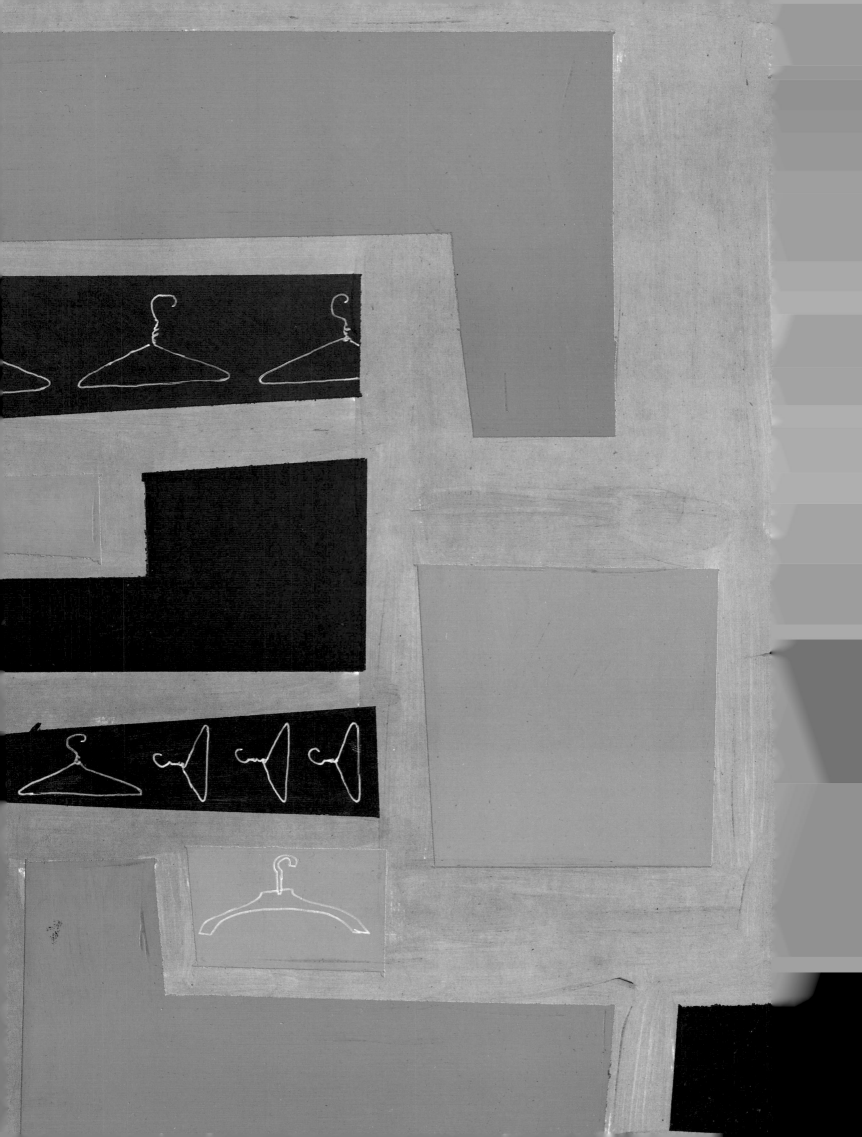

First published in Great Britain in 1999 by Bloomsbury Publishing Plc
38 Soho Square, London W1V 5DF
This paperback edition first published in 2000

Text copyright © Adrienne Geoghegan 1999
Illustrations copyright © Adrian Johnson 1999
The moral right of the author and illustrator has been asserted.

A CIP catalogue record for this book is available from the British Library.
ISBN 0 7475 4765 3 (paperback)
ISBN 0 7475 4109 5 (hardback)

Designed by Dawn Apperley
Printed and bound in Belgium by Proost NV, Turnhout.

1 3 5 7 9 10 8 6 4 2

THERE'S A WARDROBE IN MY MONSTER!

Adrienne Geoghegan and Adrian Johnson

BLOOMSBURY
CHILDREN'S
BOOKS

Martha was bored with her goldfish.
Her cat was always asleep.
And her dog couldn't do one single trick.

'What I want is a monster,' she said. 'A naughty, wicked, great big ugly monster.' So she marched into the nearest pet shop in town with all her piggy bank savings.

large monster please,' she said quite boldly.

'I'm afraid there's not enough room in here to keep large monsters,' said the pet shop man, 'but we do stock a smaller variety. Follow me.'

There were quite a lot of baby monsters at the back of the shop. 'Some of them grow huge,' said the pet shop man.

'That pink one there is a little shy, and the blue one is very cranky.'
'What about that green fellah with the awful grin?' said Martha.
'Oh him,' said the pet shop man, 'he only eats wood.'
'I'll take him,' said Martha, handing over her piggy bank.
'Keep the pig,' she said, as she left the shop with her brand new wood-eating monster.

When she got home she hid him in a shoebox in her bedroom,
and sneaked out to fetch his supper – twigs on toast.
He devoured them and wanted more.

So Martha went further down the garden, sawed some

branches off a tree, and buttered them in the kitchen.

He demolished them and demanded more.

This time Martha dismantled the dog's kennel and

spiced the planks with strong pepper.

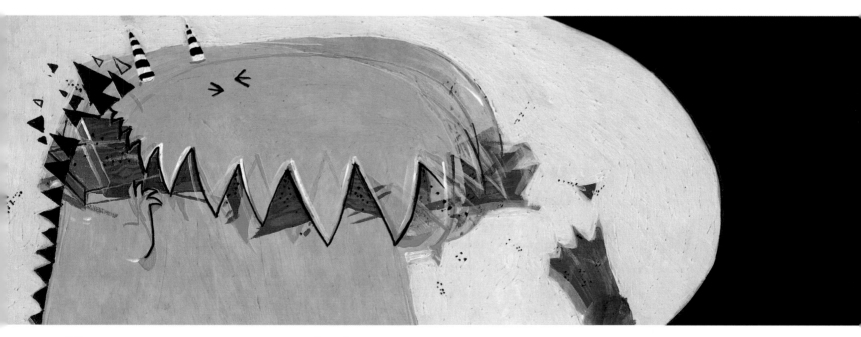

These, too, were guzzled with a grin and a burp.

Things got worse. That night Martha awoke to a terrible crunching munching sound. She sat up in the bed to listen, and slid off the edge. The monster had eaten one of the legs! 'You greedy thing!' she cried.
'How can I sleep in a three-legged bed?'

He was no longer happy with twigs on toast, buttered branches or peppered planks. He was too monstrous to fit in a shoebox or a drawer.

And there was no 'under the bed' left, as he had scoffed the other three legs!

By now he was much too big for the shoebox, so Martha shoved him into her bottom drawer – and he ate that for breakfast!

'You DESPICABLE monster!' she cried. 'Where on earth will I put my knickers?'

'Tomorrow you go on a diet,' said Martha, as she stuffed him into her wardrobe. But it was too late.

Martha was woken early next morning by a thunderous, great big belch. Her monster was MASSIVE! And her wardrobe was GONE!

'Enough is ENOUGH!'
cried Martha.
She quickly put the monster on a leash and squeezed him
out of the house. They made their way back to the pet shop.

'Excuse me sir,' she said to the pet shop man, 'but there's a wardrobe in my monster!'
'Oh, dear,' he replied; 'does he need some coat-hangers?'

Martha was furious.
'Don't be funny – and give me a refund!' she yelled.
'Very well,' said the pet shop man, 'but NO cash.'
Martha thought about her sleepy cat, bored goldfish and dopey dog.

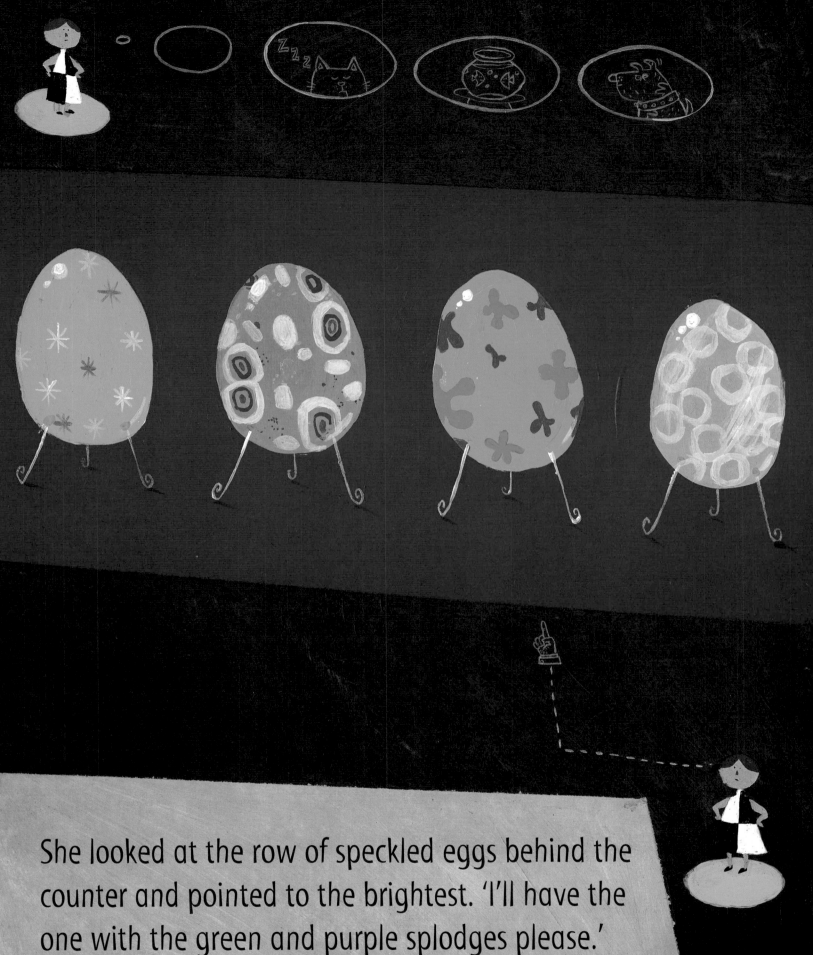

She looked at the row of speckled eggs behind the counter and pointed to the brightest. 'I'll have the one with the green and purple splodges please.' 'With all due respect Miss, I think you'd be wiser to choose . . .'

Martha thumped her little red fist on the counter,
'Now!' she growled.
The egg was carefully wrapped in tissue paper and gently
placed in a small cardboard box.
'Thank you,' smiled Martha and off she went.
The monster was squeezed out the back door.
'There's no place for you Mister Monster, but the back yard,'
said the pet shop man.

And the monster grinned his most awful grin, and had garden shed for lunch!

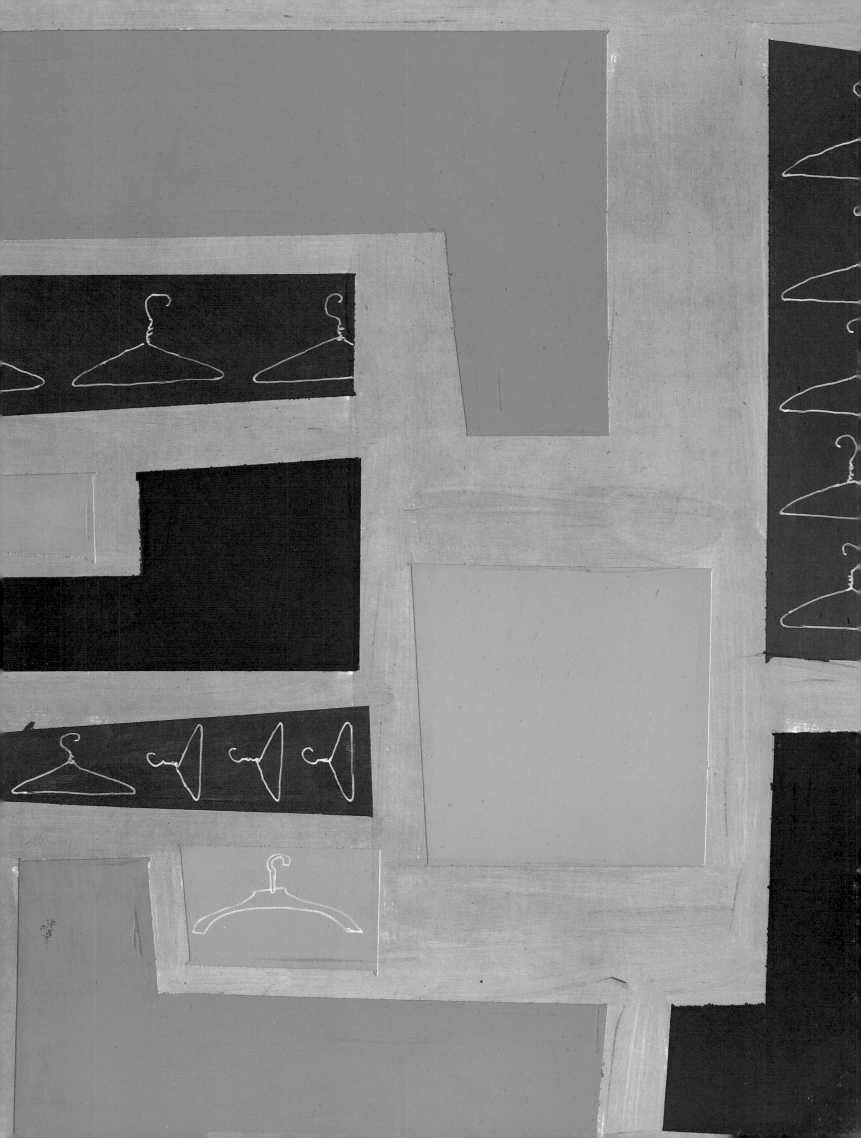

Acclaim for this book

'... we don't often see picture book illustration like
Adrian Johnson's, in which sophisticated design
is carried by simplified imagery, brilliant colour,
and elegant line' *The Times Educational Supplement*

'Adrienne Geoghegan is a clever and funny writer
who successfully manages that tricky art of talking to,
rather than at, children' *Birmingham Post*